W9-DCI-349

DOUNIA

NATACHA KARVOSKAIA

Story told by Zidrou

A CRANKY NELL BOOK

Kane/Miller Book Publishers

Brooklyn, New York & La Jolla, California

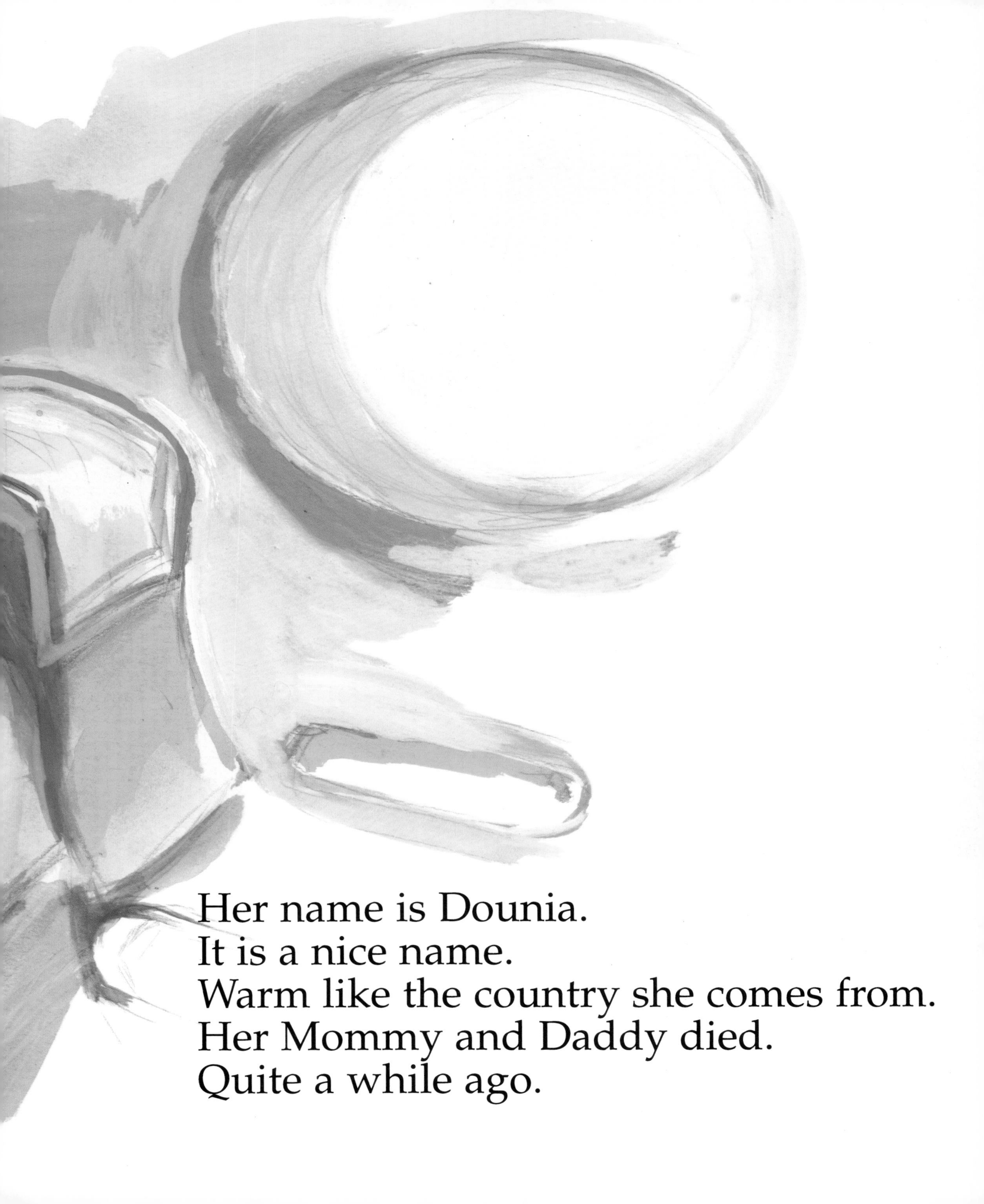

Her name is Dounia.
It is a nice name.
Warm like the country she comes from.
Her Mommy and Daddy died.
Quite a while ago.

Now Dounia has a new Mommy
and Daddy here in her new country.
Her new Mommy is called Caroline.
Her new Daddy is called Steven.

They are nice.
Their eyes shine
when they look at Dounia.
Dounia would like to greet them.
But she doesn't dare.

The car goes through a big, gray city. Caroline turns around to check that Dounia is all right. She smiles. Dounia would like to give her a smile too. But she doesn't dare.

"Home!" says Steven
"27 Daffodil Avenue.
Your house."
Dounia would like to ask
what a daffodil is.
But she doesn't dare.

Never had Dounia been in such a
big house. A house with a forest inside!
Dounia would like to run everywhere.
But she doesn't dare.

A kitchen like grocery shelves!
A living room like a bookshop!
Corridors like a museum!
Dounia would like to touch everything.
But she doesn't dare.

Dounia has a bedroom.
A bedroom just for her!
A mirror to watch herself grow.
A lamp to frighten the night.
And a bed to dream.
Dounia would like to jump on the bed.
But she doesn't dare.

Steven prepared a cake to welcome Dounia.
Caroline puts some nice music on.
Dounia would like to dance and sing.
But she doesn't dare.

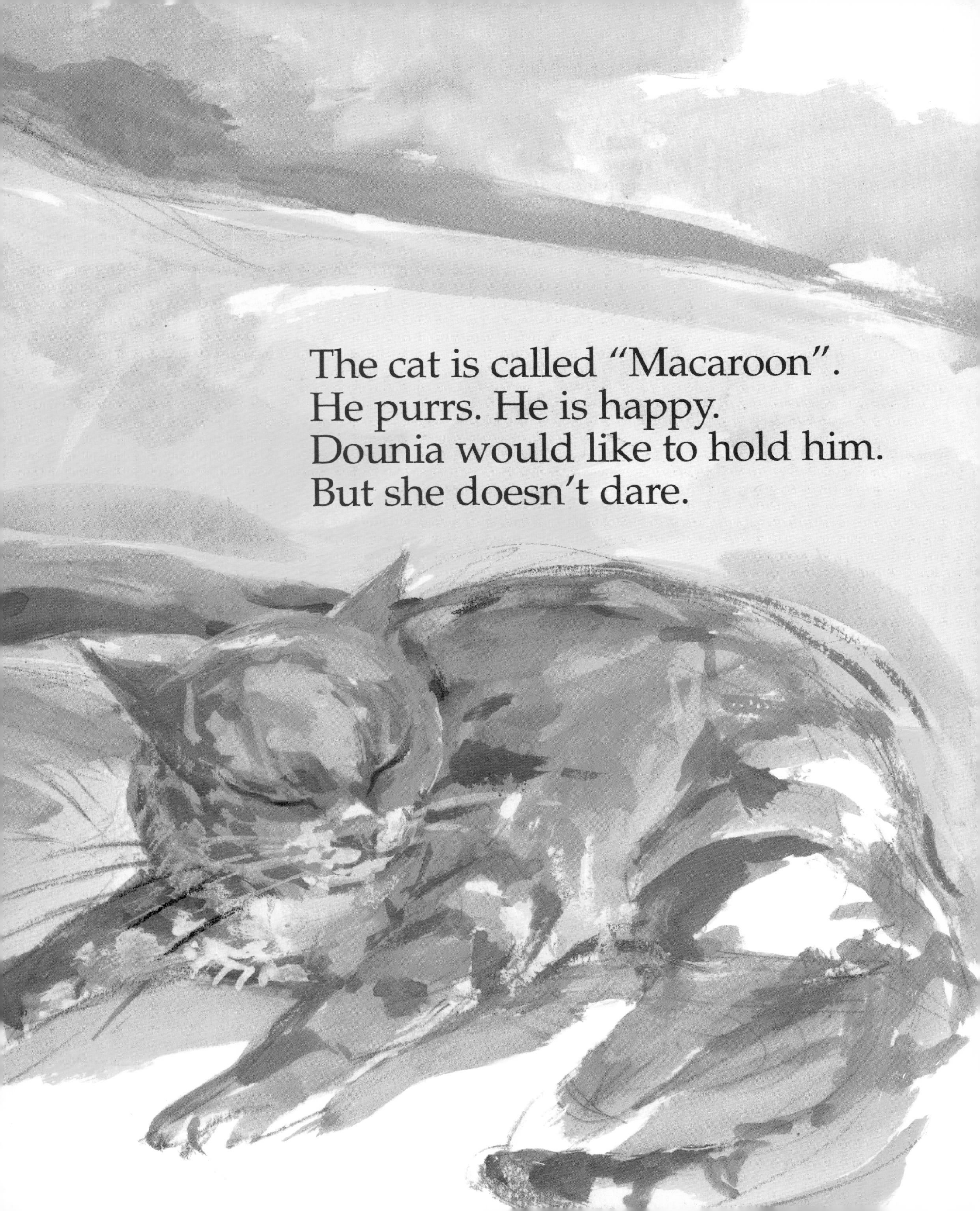

The cat is called "Macaroon".
He purrs. He is happy.
Dounia would like to hold him.
But she doesn't dare.

It's already quite late.
Caroline wishes Dounia good night and gives her a warm kiss on the forehead.
Dounia would like to give her a kiss too.
But she doesn't dare.

Tomorrow she is sure
that she will dare . . .